Enid Blyton

A FARAWAY TREE
Adventure

The Land of
BIRTHDAYS

For Alice
A. P.

EGMONT
We bring stories to life

Cover and interior illustrations by Alex Paterson

Text first published in Great Britain as chapters 27 – 29
of *The Enchanted Wood* 1939
Published as *The Land of Birthdays: A Faraway Tree Adventure* 2016
by Egmont UK Limited
The Yellow Building, 1 Nicholas Road, London W11 4AN

Text copyright © 1939 Hodder & Stoughton Ltd.
ENID BLYTON ® Copyright © 2016 Hodder & Stoughton Ltd.
ENID BLYTON ® Illustrations Copyright © 2016 Hodder & Stoughton Ltd.

ISBN 978 1 4052 8004 4

www.egmont.co.uk

A CIP catalogue record for this title is available from the British Library

Printed in Malaysia

62076/1

Enid Blyton

A FARAWAY TREE
Adventure

The Land of
BIRTHDAYS

EGMONT

The World of the FARAWAY TREE

MOON-FACE lives at the very top. In his house is the start of the **SLIPPERY-SLIP**, a huge slide that curves all the way down inside the trunk of the tree.

SILKY lives below Moon-Face. She is the prettiest little fairy you ever did see.

SAUCEPAN MAN is a funny old thing. His saucepans make lots of noise when they jangle together, so he can't hear very well.

CHAPTER ONE
Beth's Birthday

The children were on their way to the Enchanted Wood, to celebrate Beth's birthday. They knew the way to the Faraway Tree very well by now.

'**Wisha-wisha-wisha!**' whispered the trees, as the children ran between them.

Beth put her arms round one, and pressed her left ear to the trunk. '**What secret are you saying today?**' she asked.

'We wish you a happy birthday,' whispered the leaves. Beth laughed! It was fun to have a birthday!

When they came to the Faraway Tree, how marvellous it looked! The folk of the tree had bedecked it with lots of little brightly coloured flags because it was Beth's birthday, and it looked simply lovely.

'Oooh!' said Beth, pleased. 'I do feel happy. The only thing I wish is that I had **proper party clothes** on, not my old ones.'

But that couldn't be helped. They were just about to climb the tree when Dame Washalot's big washing basket came **bumping** down on the end of Moon-Face's rope for the children to get into.

'Good,' said Joe. **'Get in, girls.'**

They all got in and went up the tree at a tremendous rate. 'Moon-Face must have someone helping him to pull,' said Joe, astonished.

He had. Mister Whiskers was there, with Watzisname and the Old Saucepan Man, and they were all pulling like anything.

No wonder the basket shot up the tree!

'Many happy returns of the day,' said everyone, kissing Beth.

'**Oh, good!** You're not in your best clothes,' said Moon-Face. 'We wondered if you would make it a **fancy-dress party,** Beth.'

5

'Oh, I'd love to!'

said Beth. 'But we haven't got any fancy dress.' 'We can easily get that in the Birthday Land!' said Silky, clapping her hands for joy. 'Good, good, good! I do like a fancy-dress party!'

'Everybody is ready to go,' said Moon-Face. 'The elves are just below us. Where's Saucepan Man? **Hey, Saucepan,** where have you got to?'

'He stepped into your slippery-slip by mistake,' said an elf, appearing out of Moon-Face's house. 'He went down the slide with an awful noise. I expect he's at the bottom by now.'

'Good gracious! Just like silly Old Saucepan!' said Moon-Face. 'We'd better let down the washing basket for him, or he'll never get up to us!'

So down went the washing basket again, and Old Saucepan got into it and came up with a **clatter** of saucepans and kettles.

'Now are we **really** all ready?'
said Moon-Face. 'Silky – Watzisname
– Saucepan – the Angry Pixie – Dame
Washalot – Mister Whiskers – the elves . . .'

'Goodness! What a lovely lot of people are
coming!' said Beth, seeing all the elves and
tree-folk on the branches below. 'Is that Dame
Washalot? What a nice old woman!'

Dame Washalot was beaming happily. For
once she was going to leave her wash-tub.
Going to the Land of Birthdays was not a
treat to be missed!

'Come on, then,' said Moon-Face, and
he led the way up the ladder. Up he went,
popped his head above to make quite sure
that the Land of Birthdays was there,
and then jumped straight into it!

Everyone climbed up. 'That's all, I think,' said Moon-Face, peering down. 'Oh no – there's someone else. Whoever is it? I thought we were all here?'

'Goodness! It's my clock!' said Silky. 'The one I got in the Land of Take-What-You-Want!'

Sure enough, it was. **'Ding-dong-ding-dong!'** it cried indignantly, as it climbed up on its flat feet.

'All right, all right, we'll wait for you!' said Silky. 'Go carefully up the ladder. You weren't really asked, you know.'

'Oh, I'd love your clock
to come to my party,' said
Beth at once. **'Come along,
clock.'**

'Ding-dong,' said the
clock, pleased, and managed
to get up the ladder.

11

CHAPTER TWO
The Birthday Feast

The Land of Birthdays was simply beautiful.
To begin with, there was always birthday
weather there — brilliant sunshine, blue sky,
and a nice little breeze. The trees were always
green, and there were always daisies and
buttercups growing in the fields.

'Oh, it's lovely, it's lovely!' cried Beth,

12

dancing around joyfully. 'Moon-Face, what about our fancy dress? Where do we get that?'

'Oh, you'll find everything in that house over there,' said Moon-Face, pointing to a very pretty house.

They all trooped over to it. As they went, small brown rabbits hopped out of holes, called **'A Happy Birthday!'** to Beth, and popped back inside. It was all very exciting.

13

Everyone crowded into the pretty house. It was full of cupboards – and in the cupboards were the most thrilling costumes you can think of.

'**Oh, look at this!**' cried Joe, as he came across a sailor's outfit, with a smart hat that had blue, white and gold on it, just like the captain of a ship. 'Just the right size for me!'

He put it on. Beth chose a dress like a fairy's, and Frannie chose a clown's costume with a pointed hat. She looked just like the real thing.

Moon-Face dressed up as a pirate and Silky became a daffodil. Watzisname was a policeman, and as for the Old Saucepan Man, he simply could not find a costume to fit him, because he was so bumpy with kettles and saucepans!

Everyone else dressed up and, **oh my,** they did look convincing! Beth had wings with her dress, but she was disappointed because she couldn't fly with them. How she would have loved to spread her wings and fly, as the real fairies did!

'Now for **balloons!**' said Silky, and she danced into the sunshine and ran to an old balloon-seller who was sitting surrounded by a great cloud of coloured balloons. Everybody chose one, and what games they had!

Suddenly a bell rang, and Moon-Face gave a shout of joy. **'Birthday feast! Come on, everyone!'**

He rushed to a long, long table set out in the field. Beth ran with the others, and took her place at the head of the table. But to her great surprise and disappointment there was no food on the table at all – just empty plates, cups, and glasses!

'Don't look so upset!' whispered Silky.
'You've got to wish your own birthday feast!'

Beth gave a squeak. Wish her own birthday feast! **Oooh!** That would be the best fun in the world!

'Don't wish for bread and butter!' called Moon-Face. **'Wish for an ice-cream sundae,** I like those!'

'I wish for an ice-cream sundae!' said Beth at once. And immediately the biggest, tallest sundae you ever saw appeared on one of the empty plates. Moon-Face helped himself.

'Wish for strawberries and ice-cream!'
cried Frannie, who simply loved that.

'I wish for strawberries and ice-cream!'
said Beth, and an enormous dish of
strawberries appeared, with a large tub of
vanilla ice-cream beside it. 'And I wish for
chocolate cake too – and – and . . .'

'**Fruit salad!**' yelled someone.

'**Doughnuts!**' cried Watzisname.

'**Cheese sandwiches!**' begged Mister Whiskers.

'**Ding-dong-ding-dong!**' said Silky's clock in the greatest excitement. Everyone laughed.

'Don't wish for ding-dongs!' said Joe. 'We've got plenty of those, as long as Silky's clock is here!'

The clock chimed fourteen times without stopping. It wandered about, looking as happy as could be.

Everyone began to eat. **My goodness,** it was a wonderful feast!

The strawberries and ice-cream and the sundae went almost at once, for Mister Whiskers and fifty elves decided that they liked those very much too! So Beth had to wish for some more.

'What about my birthday cake?' she asked Silky. 'Do I wish for that too?'

'No, it just comes,' said Silky. 'It will appear right in the middle of the table. **You just watch.'**

Beth watched. There was a wonderful silver dish in the middle of the table. Something seemed to be forming there. A curious sort of mist hung over it.

'The birthday cake is coming!' shouted Joe, and everyone watched the silver dish. Gradually a great cake shaped itself there – oh, a wonderful cake, with red, pink, white, and yellow decorations made from sugar, and shaped like little flowers.

On the top were eight candles burning, for Beth was eight that day. Her name was written in big sugar letters on the top:

Beth. A very happy birthday!

Beth felt very proud. She had to cut the cake, of course. It was quite a difficult job, for there were so many people to cut a slice for.

'This is a wishing-cake!' said Moon-Face, when everyone had a piece on their plate. 'So wish, **wish, wish,** when you eat it – and your wish will come true!'

The children stared at him in delight. What should they wish?

Frannie was just holding her cake in her hand, thinking of a wish, when the Old Saucepan Man upset everything! Whatever do you think he did?

CHAPTER THREE
The Little Lost Island

'Wouldn't you like to wish?' said Moon-Face, turning to the Old Saucepan Man, who was just about to bite into his cake.

'Fish?' said the Saucepan Man, in delight. 'Yes, I'd love to fish! I wish we were all fishing for fine fat fishes in the middle of the sea.'

Well! What a wish to make, just as he was eating a wishing-cake, for he hadn't heard Moon-Face properly. Anyway, the wish immediately came true. A wind blew down, and lifted up the whole crowd of guests at the table.

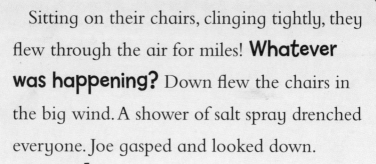

Sitting on their chairs, clinging tightly, they
flew through the air for miles! **Whatever
was happening?** Down flew the chairs in
the big wind. A shower of salt spray drenched
everyone. Joe gasped and looked down.

Bump! He and everyone else landed on
soft sand, rolled off their chairs, and sat up,
blinking in surprise.

The long-bearded elves looked frightened.

Moon-Face kept opening and shutting his mouth like a fish, he was so astonished. Joe was cross, and so was the Angry Pixie.

'**Now what's happened?**' said Dame Washalot, in a most annoyed voice. '**Why have we come here?**'

'Look at all those fishing-rods!' said Silky.

She pointed to a whole row of rods standing in the sand, with their fishing lines in the water.

'Waiting for us!' groaned Moon-Face. 'Silly Old Saucepan Man didn't hear what I said about wishing – he thought I said fishing – and he wished us all here, fishing in the sea!'

'Goodness!' said Beth, alarmed. **'Where are we, then?'**

'I think we're on the Little Lost Island,' said Silky, looking round. 'It's a funny little place, always floating about and getting lost. But there's always good fishing to be had from it.'

'Fishing!' said Joe, in disgust. 'Who wants to go fishing in the middle of a birthday party? Let's get back at once.'

'Ding-dong-ding-dong!' said Silky's clock, walking about at the edge of the sea and getting its feet wet in the waves.

'**Come back, clock!**' called Silky.
'**You know you can't swim.**'

The clock came back and wiped its feet on the grass that grew around. Beth thought it was a remarkably sensible clock, and she wished she had one like it.

'You know, we really must do something about getting back to the Land of Birthdays,' said Joe, getting up and looking around the little island. **'What can we do?** Is there a boat here?'

There was nothing except the fishing rods!
Nobody even touched them, for they didn't
feel in the least like fishing. The Little Lost
Island was just a hilly stretch of green grass
and nothing else whatsoever.

'I really don't know **what** to do!'
said Moon-Face, frowning. 'Do you, Mister
Whiskers?'

Mister Whiskers was dressed up like Santa Claus, and looked very fine indeed, with his long beard. He rubbed his nose thoughtfully and shook his head.

'The difficulty is,' he said, 'that none of us has any **magic** with him, because we're all in fancy dress and our other clothes are in the Land of Birthdays. So the spells and magic we keep in our pockets are not here.'

'Well, we shan't starve,' said Watzisname. 'We can always fish.'

'Fancy eating fish and nothing but fish always!' said Joe, making a face. 'When I think of all those lovely things that Beth wished for – and nobody to eat them now! **Really, I could cry!'**

Frannie had something in her hand and she looked down to see what it was. It was a piece of the birthday cake. Good! She could eat that, at any rate.

She lifted the **delicious cake** to her mouth and took a nibble.

'What are you eating?' asked Moon-Face, bending over to see.

'A bit of the birthday cake,' said Frannie, cramming all of it into her mouth.

'**Don't eat it!** Don't swallow it!'
yelled Moon-Face suddenly, dancing round
Frannie as if he had gone quite mad. '**Stop!
Don't swallow!**'

Frannie stared at him in astonishment. So
did everyone else.

'What's gone wrong with Moon-Face?'
asked Silky anxiously. Frannie stood still with

34

her mouth full of birthday cake, looking with amazement at Moon-Face.

'What's the matter?' she asked with her mouth full.

'You've got a bit of the wishing-cake in your mouth, Frannie!' shouted Moon-Face, hopping first on one leg and then on the other. **'Wish, dear girl, wish!'**

'**What shall I wish?**' said Frannie.

'Wish us back to the Land of Birthdays, of course!' yelled everyone in excitement.

'**Oh,**' said Frannie, '**I didn't think of that!** I wish we were all back in the Land of Birthdays, enjoying our feast!'

CHAPTER FOUR
Wishes for Everyone

Darkness fell round everyone very suddenly. No wind came this time. Moon-Face put out his hand and took Silky's. **What was happening?**

Then daylight came back again – and everyone gave a shout of surprise and delight. They were back in the Land of Birthdays!

Yes – there was the table in front of them and more chairs to sit down on, and the same delicious food as before!

'Oh, good, good, good!' shouted everyone, and sat down at once. They beamed at one another, very thankful to be back from the Little Lost Island.

'What a strange little adventure!'
said Joe, helping himself to a large piece of
wishing-cake. 'Please be careful what you
wish, everybody – we don't want any more
adventures like that in the middle of a party!'

'I wish that my wings could fly!' said Beth,
as she munched her cake. And at once her
wings spread themselves out, and she rose into
the air like a big butterfly, flying beautifully.
Oh, it was the loveliest feeling in the world!
'Look at me – look at me!' she
cried – and everyone looked.

Frannie called out to her. 'Don't fly
too far, Beth. Don't fly too far!'

Beth soon flew down to the table again,
her cheeks red with excitement and joy.
This was the **loveliest birthday party**
she had ever had!

Everybody wished their wishes except the Old Saucepan Man, who had already wasted his.

Frannie, too, had wished her wish when she was on the Little Lost Island, but when she looked upset because she had lost her wish, Moon-Face whispered to her.

'**Don't be upset.** Tell me what you really wanted to wish and I'll wish it for you. I don't want a wish for myself.'

'Oh, **Moon-Face, you are kind!**' said Frannie. 'Well, if you really mean it, I did want a doll that could walk and talk.'

'**Easy!**' said Moon-Face at once. 'I wish that Frannie had a doll that walks and talks.'

And at that very moment Silky cried out in wonder and pointed behind her. **Everyone looked.** Coming along on small, plump legs was a doll, beautifully dressed in blue, with a bag in its hand.

It walked to Frannie and looked up at her.
'Oh! You lovely, beautiful doll!' cried
Frannie in the greatest delight, and she lifted
the doll on to her knee.

It cuddled up to her and
said, 'I belong to you. I am
your own doll. My name
is Peronel.'

'What a sweet name!' said Frannie, hugging the doll. 'What have you got in that bag, Peronel?'

'All my other clothes,' said the doll, and opened her bag. Inside were nightdresses, a dressing-gown, an overcoat, a raincoat, overalls, dresses, and all kinds of other clothes. Frannie was simply delighted.

'What did you wish, Joe?' asked Beth. Joe was looking all round and about as if he expected something to arrive at any moment.

'I wished for a pony of my own,' said Joe. **'Oh!** Look! Here it comes! **What a beauty!'**

A little black pony, with a white mark on its forehead and four white feet, came trotting up to the party. It went straight to Joe.

'My own little pony!' cried the little boy, in delight. 'Let me ride you! I shall call you **Midnight Star** – for the little white star on your black coat.'

He jumped on the pony's back and together
they went galloping round the Land of
Birthdays.

'Now let's play games!' cried Moon-Face,
capering about. And as soon as he said that,
the table vanished and music began to play.
'Musical chairs! Musical chairs!'
shouted Silky, as the chairs suddenly put
themselves together in a long row. 'Come
on, everybody!'

CHAPTER FIVE

Games and Presents

The party went on and on. The game
of musical chairs was fun, for instead of
somebody taking a chair away each time
the music stopped, the chair took itself away,
walked neatly off, and stood watching.

Silky won that game. She was so quick and
light on her feet. A **big box of chocolates**
came flying down through the air to her,

when she sat down on the very last chair and pushed Moon-Face away! She was delighted. **'Let's all have one!'** she said, and opened the box at once. Whilst they were eating they saw a most astonishing sight.

47

'**Look!**' said Moon-Face, almost swallowing his chocolate in astonishment. '**What's this coming?**'

Everyone looked. It seemed like a lot of little brightly coloured men, running very upright. What do you suppose they were?

'Birthday presents!' shouted
Watzisname, jumping off his seat in delight.
'Presents – running to us – ready to be
unwrapped!'

Really, those presents were the **greatest fun!** They were like little gift-wrapped boxes on tiny legs, dodging away, trying not to be caught! Everyone ran after them, laughing and shouting.

One by one the happy little boxes were caught, and then they were unwrapped and opened. **My goodness**, what special things there were inside!

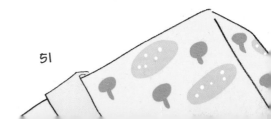

'I've got a brooch in the shape of the Faraway Tree!' cried Frannie, pinning it on herself.

'I want one too,' said her doll.

'Well, you must catch a present then, Peronel,' said Frannie, and how she laughed to see her doll running about after a red birthday-present box!

Peronel caught one at last and brought it back to Frannie. Inside there was a teddy-bear shaped brooch, which Peronel was simply delighted with!

Joe found a **shining silver whistle** inside his present. When he blew, it sounded just like all the birds in the Enchanted Wood. He was very happy with it.

Moon-Face found a special squeaker that sounded just like a cat mewing, and made the Old Saucepan Man go hunting for cats all the time! **Naughty Moon-Face!** He pressed his squeaker behind the Saucepan Man and laughed till he cried to hear him calling, **'Puss! Puss! Puss!'** and looking under tables and chairs.

Silky's clock wanted a present too. So it ran
after one, and trod on one to catch it. It held
it with its foot and unwrapped it with Silky.
What do you suppose was in it? A tiny
can of oil!

'Just the thing to oil your clockwork wheels
and springs with!' said Silky in delight.

The clock was very pleased. It **chimed
twenty-two times** without stopping,
much to the walking doll's astonishment.

They played **hide-and-seek,** and immediately the most exciting bushes and trees sprang up everywhere to hide behind. Really, the Birthday Land was the most exciting country to be in!

Then they played pin-the-tail-on-the-donkey – and a **giant toy donkey** and a big fluffy tail appeared out of nowhere!

Then they thought they would have races –
and, hey presto! – they saw a crowd of
small cars drive up, all ready to be raced.

In got everyone, choosing the car they liked
best. There was even a tiny one for Peronel
the doll, and an extra one for Silky's clock,
who joined in the fun and **ding-donged**
merrily all the time.

The Old Saucepan Man won the race, though he dropped a few saucepans on the way. Moon-Face handed him a box of toffee that had appeared for the winner.

'You've won!' he said.

'Run?' said the Saucepan Man.

'All right, I'll run!' And he ran and ran, just to show how fast he could run when he wanted to. What a noise he made, with his kettles and saucepans clattering all round him!

'Supper-time, supper-time!' shouted Moon-Face suddenly, and he pointed to a lovely sight. About a hundred toadstools had suddenly grown up, and appearing on them were jugs of all kinds of delicious drinks, and cakes and fruit. Smaller toadstools grew beside the big ones.

'They are for seats!' cried Silky, sitting down on one and helping herself to some acornade. **'I'm hungry! Come on, everyone!'**

Beth flew down from the air. She did love flying. Frannie ran up with her doll, who followed her everywhere, talking in her little high voice. Joe galloped up on his pony. **Everyone was very happy.**

CHAPTER SIX

Safe Back Home Again

It began to get dark, but nobody minded, because big lanterns suddenly shone out everywhere in the trees and bushes. As they sat and ate, there came a loud **bang-bang!**

Peronel cuddled up to Frannie, frightened. Silky's clock tried to get on Silky's knee, scared, but she pushed it off.

62

'What's that?' said Joe, patting his frightened pony.

'Fireworks! **Fireworks!**' shouted the Angry Pixie in delight. **'Look! Look!'**

And there, in front of them, were the fireworks, setting themselves off beautifully.

Rockets **flew** high and **sizzled** down in coloured stars. Firework wheels **whizzed** round and round. Firecrackers **popped** and **banged** and **jumped** around. It was splendid to watch!

'This is the loveliest birthday party I've ever heard of,' said Beth happily, flapping her big wings, as she sat and watched the fireworks. 'Lovely things to eat – wishes that come true – exciting games – splendid presents – and now fireworks.'

'We have to go home at midnight,' said
Moon-Face, pushing away Silky's clock, which
was trying to sit on his toadstool with him.

'How shall we know when it's midnight?'
asked Frannie, thinking that it really was time
her doll went to bed.

They knew all right – because when midnight came Silky's clock stood up and chimed loudly, twelve times.

DONG - DONG - DONG - DONG - DONG - DONG - DONG - DONG - DONG - DONG - DONG - DONG!

'To the ladder!
To the ladder!' cried
Moon-Face, hurrying everyone
there. 'The Birthday Land will
soon be on the move!'

The ladder was there. Everyone
climbed down it and called goodbye.

The elves took cushions and slid off
down the slippery-slip. Mister Whiskers got
his beard caught round one of the legs of
Moon-Face's sofa and nearly took that with
him down the slide. Moon-Face just stopped it
in time, and unwound his beard.

'What about my pony?' asked Joe
anxiously. 'Do you suppose he will mind
sliding down, Moon-Face?'

'Well, he can't climb down the tree, and
he certainly wouldn't like going down in the

washing basket,' said Moon-Face.

So they sat the surprised pony on a cushion and he slid down in the **greatest astonishment**, wondering what in the world was happening to him!

Frannie slid down with her sleepy doll on her knee. Beth carefully took off her wings and folded them up. She didn't want to have them spoilt. She wanted to use them every day. She was very proud of them.

70

The pony arrived on the cushion of moss quite safely. Joe mounted him. It was dark in the wood, but the moon was just rising, and they would be able to see their way home quite well.

'**Goodbye!**' called Moon-Face from the top of the tree. '**We've had a lovely time!**'

'**Goodbye!**' called Silky.

'**Ding-dong!**' said her clock sleepily.

'**Take care of yourselves!**' shouted Watzisname.

Moon-Face pressed his squeaker loudly, and then giggled to hear the Saucepan Man call, 'Puss! Puss! Puss! Wherever is that cat!'

Slishy-sloshy-slishy-sloshy! Good gracious, was that Dame Washalot doing washing already?

Joe dodged away on his pony and the girls ran from the tree. Mister Whiskers got the water all over him, for he was standing nearby, and he was most upset.

'**Come on, girls!**' said Joe, laughing. 'We really must go home! We shall never wake up in the morning!'

So they went home once more, through the Enchanted Wood, with the moon shining pale and cold between the trees.

'**wisha-wisha-wisha!**' whispered the leaves.

Joe put his pony into the field outside the cottage. Frannie undressed Peronel and put her into her doll's bed. Beth put her wings carefully into a drawer. They all undressed and got sleepily into bed.

'Goodnight!' they said. 'What a lovely day it's been. **We are lucky to live near the Enchanted Wood!'**

They were, weren't they? Perhaps they will have more adventures one day; but now we must say goodbye to them, and leave them fast asleep, dreaming of the Land of Birthdays, and **all the lovely things** that happened there!